Kate DiCamillo
Mercy Watson
Goes for a Ride

illustrated by *Chris Van Dusen*

NO LONGER PROPERTY
OF ANYTHING
RANGEVIEW LIBRARY
DISTRICT

CANDLEWICK PRESS

D0017846

Text copyright © 2006 by Kate DiCamillo
Illustrations copyright © 2006 by Chris Van Dusen

All rights reserved. No part of this book may be reproduced, transmitted,
or stored in an information retrieval system in any form or by any means,
graphic, electronic, or mechanical, including photocopying, taping, and
recording, without prior written permission from the publisher.

First paperback edition 2009

The Library of Congress has cataloged the hardcover edition as follows:

Mercy Watson goes for a ride / by Kate DiCamillo ;
illustrated by Chris Van Dusen. —1st ed.
p. cm.
Summary: Mr. Watson's usual Saturday drive in his convertible with his favorite
pig, Mercy, turns into an adventure when an unexpected passenger shows up
in the back seat and Mercy finds herself behind the wheel.
ISBN 978-0-7636-2332-6 (hardcover)
[1. Pigs—Fiction. 2. Automotive driving—Fiction. 3. Humorous stories.]
I. Van Dusen, Chris, ill. II. Title.
PZ7.D5455Me2006
[Fic]—dc22   2004051832

ISBN 978-0-7636-4505-2 (paperback)

18 19 20 21 22 CCP 30 29 28 27 26 25

Printed in Shenzhen, Guangdong, China

This book was typeset in Mrs. Eaves.
The illustrations were done in gouache.

Candlewick Press
99 Dover Street
Somerville, Massachusetts 02144

visit us at www.candlewick.com

For Henry, who is a true menace behind the wheel

K. D.

To my four brothers and all of the rides we took together
jammed in the back of the station wagon

C. V.

Chapter
1

Mr. Watson and Mrs. Watson have a pig named Mercy.

Every Saturday, Mrs. Watson makes a special lunch.

"Time for our little Saturday Something," Mrs. Watson says.

"You've outdone yourself, Mrs. Watson," Mr. Watson says.

"Oink!" says Mercy.

Every Saturday after lunch, Mr.
Watson goes outside.

Mercy follows him.

They stand in the driveway.

Together, they admire Mr. Watson's
convertible.

"Are you ready?" asks Mr. Watson.

"Oink!" says Mercy.

Mr. Watson opens the passenger door. Mercy hops into the car.

She sits behind the wheel.

She snuffles contentedly.

Chapter
2

"Heh, heh, heh," says Mr. Watson every Saturday. "You, my dear, are a porcine wonder. But even porcine wonders cannot drive cars."

Mr. Watson gently pushes Mercy toward the passenger seat.

But Mercy does not move.

She does not want to sit in the
passenger seat.

Mercy Watson wants to drive.

"Heh, heh, heh," says Mr. Watson
again.

He pushes less gently.

"Scoot over, my dear."

Mercy does not move.

Mr. Watson calls out.

Every Saturday, Mrs. Watson steps
outside.

"Darling," Mrs. Watson says, "if you let Mr. Watson drive, I will make you an extra helping of hot buttered toast. I will have it waiting for you when you get back home."

Mercy narrows her eyes.

She loves hot buttered toast.
She also loves extra helpings.

Slowly, very slowly, she moves over to the passenger side.

"What a dear," says Mrs. Watson. She claps her hands. "You are such a good sport, darling."

"Yes," says Mr. Watson. "She most certainly is."

He gets in the car and sits behind the wheel.

He turns the key in the ignition.

The Watson convertible rumbles to life.

Chapter 3

"Bon voyage!"

Mrs. Watson calls. "*Bon voyage*, my dears! When you get home, we will all have hot buttered toast."

"Goodbye, Mrs. Watson!" Mr. Watson shouts.

He backs the car out of the driveway very quickly.

He does not look behind him.

Mr. Watson is a forward-looking man. He does not believe in looking back.

"Oink," says Mercy. Already she is having a good time.

"And we're off," says Mr. Watson. "We're off on an adventure!"

Chapter
4

Eugenia Lincoln and Baby Lincoln live next door to the Watsons.

Every Saturday, the Lincoln Sisters watch Mercy and Mr. Watson back out of the driveway.

Every Saturday, Eugenia is displeased.

"Mr. Watson is a very bad driver," she says. "He is a menace behind the wheel."

"Yes, Sister," says Baby.

"Furthermore," says Eugenia, "it is my firm opinion that pigs should not be taken for rides in automobiles. Particularly *that* pig. *That* pig is a sly pig. I do not trust her."

"No, Sister," says Baby.

Baby looks down the road.

The car has disappeared.

Mr. Watson and Mercy are gone.

"Folly," says Eugenia Lincoln. She shakes her fist. "It is folly, I say."

"Yes, Sister," says Baby.

But secretly, Baby Lincoln thinks that a little folly wouldn't be a bad thing.

Chapter
5

One Saturday, Mrs. Watson made a special lunch.

After lunch, Mr. Watson and Mercy went outside.

Everything happened just as it always did every Saturday on Deckawoo Drive.

"What folly," said Eugenia Lincoln, as usual. "What nonsense."

She paused.

Eugenia waited for Baby to say,
"Yes, Sister."

But Baby said nothing.

Baby said nothing because Baby
was not there.

Chapter
6

Officer Tomilello sat in his police cruiser.

A pink convertible sped past him.

"Was that a pig?" Officer Tomilello asked himself.

"Yes, it was," he answered himself. "That most certainly was a pig."

"Is it illegal to take a pig for a ride?"
Officer Tomilello asked himself.

"I don't believe it is," he answered
himself.

"It is unusual," he continued. "But
unusual does not equal illegal. However,
it *is* illegal to speed. And that vehicle
was definitely speeding."

Officer Tomilello turned on his
flashing lights. He pulled out onto the
highway.

He followed the car with the pig
in it.

Chapter
7

In the car with the pig in it, the pig was having a very good time.

The wind was tickling her ears.

The sun was warm on her snout.

Even though she was not the one behind the wheel, Mercy was happy.

Mr. Watson was happy, too.

"There's nothing like a fast drive to
clear the mind!" he shouted. "Isn't
that right, my dear?"

"Oink," said Mercy.

"It *is* wonderful to go fast," said a voice from the back seat.

"Who said that?" said Mr. Watson.

"Me," said Baby Lincoln.

Mr. Watson looked over his shoulder.

"Hello, Mr. Watson," said Baby.

"Oink!" said Mercy.

"Hello, Mercy," said Baby.

"What are you doing?" shouted Mr. Watson.

"I am having a little adventure," said Baby. "I am indulging in some folly."

"Folly?" said Mr. Watson.

Mercy narrowed her eyes.

Mr. Watson was looking over his shoulder at Baby. He was not looking at the road.

Mercy saw her chance.

She gathered her strength.

She leaped.

"Help," Mr. Watson said. "Help
me!"

"Whooooeeeeeeeee," said Baby Lincoln. "What folly, what fun, what adventure!"

"Please," said Mr. Watson, "get off me."

He pushed at Mercy with both hands.

But Mercy did not move.

She put her front hooves on the steering wheel.

She was in the driver's seat.

And she intended to stay there.

Chapter
8

Back on Deckawoo Drive, Eugenia
Lincoln was looking for Baby.

She looked in Baby's bed.

Baby was not there.

She looked on the back step.

Baby was not there, either.

"BABY!" shouted Eugenia. "Reveal yourself at once!"

But Baby did not reveal herself.

"Where could she be?" said Eugenia. "And why do I think this has something to do with that *pig*?"

Eugenia marched next door.

She rang the Watsons' bell.

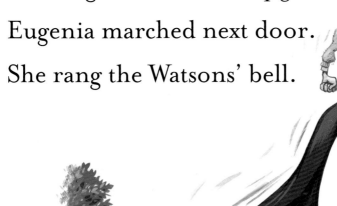

"Mrs. Watson," said Eugenia, "Baby is missing."

"Goodness," said Mrs. Watson.

"And I believe that your pig is responsible," said Eugenia.

"Mercy?" said Mrs. Watson.

"Yes," said Eugenia, "exactly."

"But Mercy is not here," said Mrs. Watson. "She is on her Saturday ride with Mr. Watson."

Eugenia turned and looked down the road.

"Folly!" she said.

"Heavens," said Mrs. Watson. "You
don't think . . ."

"I do think," said Eugenia. "That is
my point exactly. I do think. And
apparently, I am the only one around
here who does."

Chapter
9

Officer Tomilello had to go very fast to catch up with the convertible.

The officer had to speed.

"Is that vehicle swerving?" Officer Tomilello asked himself.

"It is," he answered himself. "It is most definitely swerving."

"Is the driver of that vehicle breaking the law?" Officer Tomilello asked.

"Without a doubt," he answered, "the law is being broken. It is time to take action."

Officer Tomilello pulled up alongside the car. He shouted into his bullhorn:

PULL OVER!

The driver turned.

The driver looked at him.

The driver oinked.

"Is that pig . . . behind the wheel?" Officer Tomilello asked himself.

"Yes," he answered himself. "Yes, that pig is most definitely behind the wheel."

Again Officer Tomilello shouted into his bullhorn.

"**PULL OVER! PIGS CANNOT DRIVE CARS. PULL OVER IMMEDIATELY!**"

"He is absolutely correct," said Mr. Watson. "Pigs cannot drive cars. And I would like to pull over. But I can no longer feel my legs. Therefore, I cannot step on the brake pedal. Therefore, I cannot stop this car."

"Oh, dear," said Baby. "I think we are in trouble."

Chapter
10

Back on Deckawoo Drive, Mrs. Watson invited Eugenia inside.

"There's no point in worrying alone," Mrs. Watson said. "Come in and help me fix a snack for my darlings."

Mrs. Watson brought Eugenia into the kitchen.

"Will you help me butter some toast?" asked Mrs. Watson.

"Toast?" grumbled Eugenia. "Who cares about toast?"

"Don't worry," said Mrs. Watson. She patted Eugenia on the back. "If Baby is with Mr. Watson, then she is just fine. Mr. Watson is an excellent driver."

"He is a *menace*," said Eugenia.

"Pardon?" said Mrs. Watson.

"Nothing," said Eugenia.

She picked up a piece of toast.

She applied the tiniest amount of butter.

"Oh, heavens," said Mrs. Watson. "You have to put on more than that. Mercy likes a great deal of butter on her toast."

"Who cares how pigs like their toast?" Eugenia said.

"There, there," said Mrs. Watson. "I know that you are worried. But everything will work out. Baby will come home. In the meantime, why don't we just concentrate on our buttering?"

"Toast is not the answer," grumbled Eugenia.

But she buttered another piece anyway.

Chapter
11

"YOU MUST STOP THE CAR!"

shouted Officer Tomilello.

"But I cannot stop the car," said

Mr. Watson.

"OINK-OINK!" said Mercy.

She was having an excellent time.

"I have an idea, Mr. Watson," said
Baby Lincoln. "If you tell me where
the brake pedal is, I will apply it."

"The brake pedal," said Mr. Watson
from underneath Mercy, "is the pedal
to the left of the gas pedal. The brake
pedal is the pedal that I do *not* have my
foot on."

Baby unbuckled her seat belt.

She climbed into the front seat.

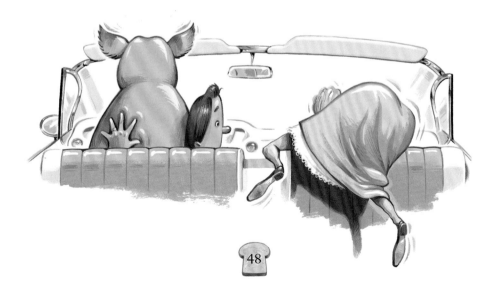

She put her seat belt on.

She slid as close to Mr. Watson as
she could.

She looked down.

She saw Mr. Watson's foot.

She saw the pedal next to it.

"I have located the brake pedal, Mr. Watson!" Baby announced.

"Excellent," said Mr. Watson. "Now apply it."

Baby stretched across Mr. Watson.

"I am applying the brake pedal, Mr. Watson!" Baby shouted. "Hold on! Hold on, everyone!"

Chapter
12

The car screeched.

The car shuddered.

The car careened.

The car caromed.

And finally, the car stopped.

Mercy was very surprised.

Suddenly, she was not driving the car.

Suddenly, she was not even *in* the car.

Suddenly, Mercy was airborne.

Mr. Watson was wearing his seat belt.

He did not fly out of the car.

Baby Lincoln was wearing her seat belt.

She did not fly out of the car.

Officer Tomilello was safe in his police cruiser.

He did not fly out of his car.

Only Mercy flew.

"Oh, dear," said Baby.

"It's an emergency!" shouted Mr. Watson. "Alert the fire department!"

"Was that pig wearing a seat belt?" Officer Tomilello asked.

"No," he answered himself. "That pig most certainly was not."

"Have laws been broken here?" asked Officer Tomilello.

"Most certainly, most definitely, laws have been broken here."

Mr. Watson and Baby Lincoln and Officer Tomilello watched Mercy fly.

56

They watched her land.

Mr. Watson got out of the car.

He ran to Mercy.

He wrapped his arms around her and held her tight.

"My darling, my dear," he said. "Please tell me that you are all right."

"Oink?" said Mercy.

She snuffled Mr. Watson's neck.

"Hooray!" said Baby. "She is fine."

"Oh, thank you," said Mr. Watson. "Thank you, thank you, thank you."

He bent his head and covered the tips of Mercy's ears with kisses.

"You are a miracle, a prodigy, a dear," Mr. Watson said. "You are a porcine wonder. But even porcine wonders cannot drive. In fact, porcine wonders should *never* be allowed to drive. *Ever.*"

Mercy sighed.

She was glad the ride was over.

She felt a tiny bit dizzy.

And a little bit dazed.

She wanted, very much, to go home.

Chapter
13

Eugenia Lincoln and Mrs. Watson
stood together on the Watsons' front
porch.

They watched a police car pull into
the driveway.

Mr. Watson and Mercy and Baby
Lincoln were all in the back seat.

"As I suspected," said Eugenia. "Trouble, folly. And that *pig* is right in the middle of it."

"Oh," said Mrs. Watson, "my darlings, my dears!"

She ran out to the police car.

"I am so glad that you are home. The toast was starting to get cold."

Mr. Watson and Baby Lincoln got out of the car.

"We have had something of an adventure, Mrs. Watson," Mr. Watson said.

"Yes," said Baby. "We have had an adventure, Sister."

"Folly," replied Eugenia Lincoln.

"Yes," agreed Baby Lincoln happily, "folly!"

"Laws have been broken," said Officer Tomilello.

"Pig!" shouted Eugenia.

"Excuse me?" said Officer Tomilello.

"It's all that pig's fault," said Eugenia.

She pointed at Mercy.

Mercy climbed out of the car. She put her nose up in the air.

She sniffed.

Could it be?

Yes, it was.

Toast!

Toast with a great deal of butter on it.

What could be better?

Chapter
14

Laws have been broken," said Officer
Tomilello. "Tickets must be written."

"Officer, do you like toast?" Mrs.
Watson asked.

"Toast?" said Officer Tomilello.
"Do I like toast? Why, yes I do. I do
like toast."

"Why don't you come inside and have some?" asked Mrs. Watson.

"Why don't I come inside and have some toast?" asked Officer Tomilello.

"Hmm," said Officer Tomilello, "I can't think of a reason *not* to."

"Lovely!" said Mrs. Watson. She clapped her hands together. "Right this way."

"What nonsense," grumbled Eugenia Lincoln. "Toast is not the answer."

"No, Sister," said Baby Lincoln. "But it does smell heavenly."

She took hold of Eugenia's hand.

"Well," said Eugenia, "it has been *expertly* buttered."

And so, that Saturday, Officer Tomilello and Eugenia Lincoln and Baby Lincoln and Mr. and Mrs. Watson and Mercy Watson all sat around the table together and ate hot buttered toast.

Did Mercy Watson have extra helpings?

She did.

And so did Officer Tomilello.

Kate DiCamillo is the renowned author of numerous books, including *The Tale of Despereaux* and *Flora & Ulysses,* both of which won the Newbery Medal, as well as all six books about Mercy Watson and the spin-off series about her neighbors, Tales from Deckawoo Drive. About *Mercy Watson Goes for a Ride,* she says, "A long time ago, my best friend's son, Luke Bailey, put a toy pig in a toy car and pushed the car around the living room, screaming, 'Look, look, pig taking a ride! Pig taking a ride!' This phrase was repeated with such shocking volume and intensity that it took up permanent residence in my brain. What you hold in your hands is the direct product of Luke's obsession and mine, a decade or so after the fact. Look, Luke, pig taking a ride!" Kate DiCamillo lives in Minneapolis.

Chris Van Dusen is the author-illustrator of many books, including *The Circus Ship, King Hugo's Huge Ego, Hattie & Hudson,* and *Randy Riley's Really Big Hit.* About *Mercy Watson Goes for a Ride,* he says, "I have four brothers (no sisters!), and cars were a big part of my upbringing. So when I read this story about a wild car ride, I couldn't wait to get started. I made the Watson convertible a 1959 Cadillac because I love old cars with lots of chrome, fins, and style. It was also great to visit these characters again. We're becoming good friends!" Chris Van Dusen lives in Maine.

Join MERCY WATSON
in all six of her pig tales!

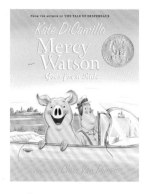

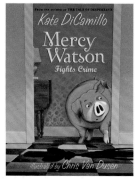

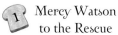 Mercy Watson
to the Rescue

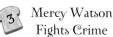 Mercy Watson
Goes for a Ride

Mercy Watson
Fights Crime

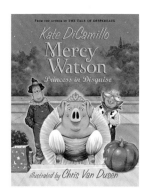

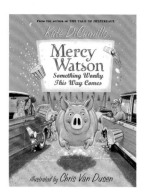

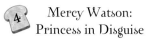 Mercy Watson:
Princess in Disguise

Mercy Watson
Thinks Like a Pig

Mercy Watson:
Something Wonky
This Way Comes

Navigate a neighborhood full of mishaps, mayhem, and a lot of hot buttered toast.

Tales from Deckawoo Drive

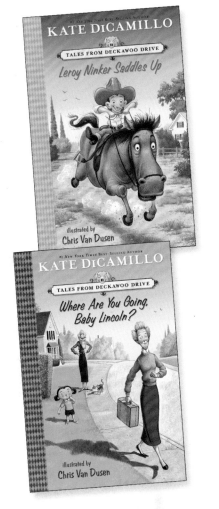